Boorityu
2011

What
Is
Peace?

VLB Veronica Lane Books

What Is Peace?

By Etan Boritzer   Illustrated by Jeff Vernon

Second Printing 2010

 *Veronica Lane Books*

www.veronicalanebooks.com   email: etan@veronicalanebooks.com
2554 Lincoln Blvd. Ste 142, Los Angeles, CA 90291 USA
Tel/Fax: +1 (800) 651-1001 / Intl: +1 (310) 745-0162

Library of Congress Cataloging-In-Publication Data
        Boritzer, Etan, 1950-
        What Is Peace / by Etan Boritzer
        Illustrated by Jeff Vernon -- 1st Edition
        p. cm.

SUMMARY: Presents children with an understanding of the various concepts of peace in the modern world and how an individual can achieve personal and social harmony.

Audience: Grades K - 6

ISBN 0976274346 (Hardbound)
ISBN 0976274353 (Paperback)

The Library of Congress No. 2006933160

This publication was supported in partnership with THE ART FUND CORPORATION.
www.theartfundcorporation.com

Rotaplast International builds understanding and goodwill among people and nations by providing free reconstructive cleft-palate surgery and treatment for children in need worldwide. Since 1992 Rotaplast plastic surgeons have volunteered their time and donated their skills in 16 developing nations correcting severe facial defects on over 9,500 children.

A child's life can be positively changed forever with a few hours of surgery.

Rotaplast International is a non-profit humanitarian organization.
To learn more about Rotaplast call +1.415.252.1111 or visit www.rotaplast.org.

Photojournalist Wayne Schoenfeld has chronicled the work of Rotaplast in two books, Mission to India and Almost Perfect, selected as Most Outstanding Book of 2004 by IPPY. For more information: www.wayneschoenfeld.com

Rotaplast

...to the children of the world...

What is Peace?

Is peace something outside of us,
or is peace something inside us?

Is peace something you can learn,
or is peace something we are born with?

Is peace something we can do,
or is peace just a feeling?
Or, is peace both a feeling
and something we can do?

Maybe peace is
a real nice awake kind of feeling,
not like being excited
and jumping around all over the place,
but not like being sleepy either.

Maybe peace is
a nice kind of feeling,
like just lying on your back
and watching the clouds go by.

What is Peace?

Did you ever go some place
real quiet like a deep green forest,
or a hot dry desert,
or up on a really high mountain?

If you ever go to one of those places
and you stop talking and playing around,
if you can stand or sit really still,
just for a few minutes,
maybe you can *feel* peace there.

But do you have to go
to a quiet place, far from the city
with all the cars and people
and noise and crazy stuff going on,
to feel peace?

Maybe we are born with peace
already deep inside us,
and maybe we can feel the peace
that is already deep inside us anywhere!

But is peace only a quiet thing?
Maybe peace is about more
than only being quiet.

Maybe once you were walking along
and you accidentally stepped on a quiet bug
because you didn't see it or hear it.
Does peace mean being quiet like that bug?

Maybe one night your Mom wants you
to turn off the TV early so that
you'll be fresh for school in the morning.
But maybe you want to watch another show!

Can you feel peace
if you argue with your Mom or your Dad,
or with your brother or sister, or a friend?

Can you feel peace
if you're quiet as a bug
but you don't get what you want?

Maybe we can't know what peace is
if we always have to argue
and try get everything we want.

But what if you want something
that is really simple or important to you
and that doesn't hurt anybody else—
but you aren't allowed to have it!
Should you argue then?

Like, what if there is a king of a country
and he orders people to do
only the things that *he* wants them to do,
or he doesn't let them do
any of the things that *they* want to do?

How can anybody feel peace
if somebody is bossing them around,
or being really unfair and hurtful?

Can you sometimes argue,
and still feel your peace inside?

What if the people get angry at the king,
and they don't want to do
what the king orders them to do anymore?

Can the people of that country
do something peaceful
to change the way the king thinks,
so that the king will listen to them
and change the things he does?

Maybe in your class you read about
some women and men, and even kids,
who had to live with a king
who made them do things
they didn't think were fair,
and how they wanted to be *free*
to do the things they thought were fair.

(To be *free* means that we can
think and say and do the things we like—
as long as we're fair
and don't hurt other people,
or ourselves.)

Maybe you read how those *brave* women
and men, and even kids
tried to change things in that country.

(To be *brave* means that you are not afraid
to say and do what you think and feel—
as long as you don't hurt other people.)

Maybe you read about how
the king tried to stop those brave people
and maybe he even hurt those people
when they tried to change things.

Now, when people hurt each other,
that's called *violence*,
and that's not a good thing.

Violence means that people stop talking,
or listening to each other,
or trying to understand each other—
and instead, they start to get angry
and then they start to fight and hurt each other
with nasty words, with their hands,
or even with guns!

And when grown-ups get angry and violent,
they sometimes start wars
and then they really hurt each other!

But is there a *peaceful* way to stop violence?
Yes, there is a peaceful way to stop violence—
and that's called *nonviolence.*

Nonviolence means that you talk
to somebody that hurt you
or that got you angry,
and you explain to that person
why you are feeling hurt or angry,
and that person explains
why she or he is feeling hurt or angry—
all without using nasty words or fighting.

Sometimes you can practice nonviolence
just by *compromising,*
and that means that you give up
a little bit of what you want,
and the other person gives up
a little bit of what she or he wants.

Compromising is another way to practice peace.
And sometimes after compromising,
people even become better friends
than they were before that started to fight.

So maybe we can start to feel peace,
when we each of us gives up
a little bit of what we want—
when we compromise.

But what happens
if somebody does something to you,
maybe not on purpose,
but it really hurts you or gets you angry?

What if one day at school
your friend stomps real hard on your foot—
by accident, or kind of like it's a joke?

Ouch! That can make you feel really angry,
so that you really want to stomp back hard
on your friend's foot!

How can you compromise,
or practice nonviolence on that one?

Maybe instead of getting angry at your friend
and losing your peace,
you can take a really deep breath,
and you can look real deep
into your friend's eyeballs,
and you can try to understand *why* he hurt you.

Hey, nobody says it's easy to be nonviolent!
Nobody says it's easy not to get angry
when somebody does something hurtful to you,
even if it's not on purpose.
Nobody says it easy to keep your peace.

But maybe you can tell your friend
that your foot hurts and so do your feelings.
And maybe you can ask your friend
why he did that hurtful thing to you.

Sometimes a person hurts somebody,
or hurts himself or herself,
if somebody is hurting them.

Maybe you after you talk with your friend
you find out that somebody is hurting him,
and that's why he wants to hurt other people.
Maybe you find out
that your friend really needs some help.

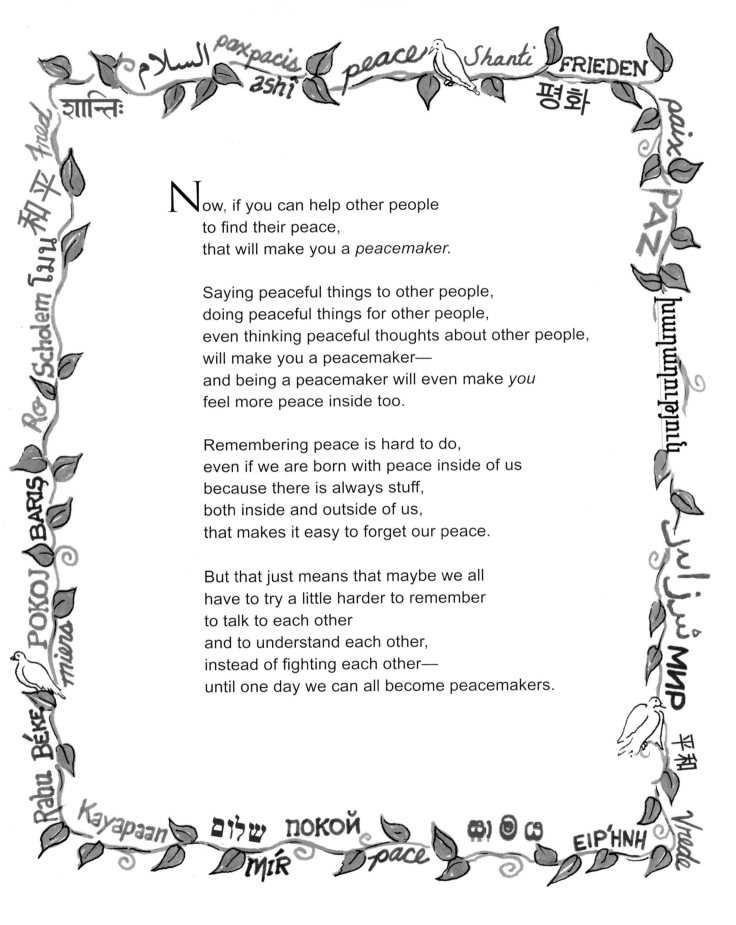

Now, if you can help other people
to find their peace,
that will make you a *peacemaker.*

Saying peaceful things to other people,
doing peaceful things for other people,
even thinking peaceful thoughts about other people,
will make you a peacemaker—
and being a peacemaker will even make *you*
feel more peace inside too.

Remembering peace is hard to do,
even if we are born with peace inside of us
because there is always stuff,
both inside and outside of us,
that makes it easy to forget our peace.

But that just means that maybe we all
have to try a little harder to remember
to talk to each other
and to understand each other,
instead of fighting each other—
until one day we can all become peacemakers.

We said that we can lose our peace
when we don't get what we want,
but how can we ever stop wanting what we want?

Sometimes we get confused
about the difference between
stuff that we *want*
and stuff that we *need.*

For instance, we need food and clothes,
and a safe house to live in, right?
We need medicine if we are sick, right?
Maybe we need a car to get to school,
and for your Mom and Dad to get to work.
Maybe we even need a few games
and some fun stuff too sometimes, right?

But suppose one day you also want
some cool new sneakers.
So, maybe you do some work
and you earn enough money
to buy those cool new sneakers you want.

But then later, maybe you see that your friend
has got some even cooler sneakers than you have!
All of a sudden you decide that
you really *want* your friend's sneakers too!

*L*ook out then!
You know you don't really *need* your friend's sneakers—
and anyway, why do you even want
that person's smelly sneakers anyway?

Can you see how crazy things can get?
If you want stuff so bad, for no good reason
and you can't get what you want,
can you see how you can lose your peace?

But lots of people will do anything—
like running around busy all day and night,
like not looking where they are going
and bumping into stuff,
like getting headaches and getting angry,
and maybe even getting violent—
just to get what they *think* they really want!

So maybe part of knowing what peace is,
is knowing the difference between
what we want and what we need—
or even just being happy with what we have.

Maybe we lose our peace
when we become afraid.

Maybe you become afraid
because you see a scary movie,
or maybe you think
there are some kind of little blue bug things
in your bed, near your feet.

Maybe you become afraid
because your friends dare you to do stuff
you don't want to do,
or maybe somebody is touching you
where he shouldn't touch you, or hurting you.

Maybe you become afraid
because your Dad and Mom are fighting,
or you think you may lose your home.

Maybe you become afraid
because somebody doesn't understand your religion,
or the language your parents speak,
or because somebody thinks about your skin color
instead of the wonderful person you really are.

Becoming afraid can make you lose your peace.

So, how can we *not* become afraid,
and not lose that nice inside feeling of peace
that we are born with
and that is always inside of us?

Sometimes people *pray* when they become afraid
and feel they are losing their peace.

To pray means that you remember
that peace is always inside of you.

And when you remember that peace
is always inside of you,
maybe you can also remember all the people
who love you and who care about you,
and who protect you,
and that will help you find your peace too.

Once you find your peace again,
you can become real strong,
and you won't be afraid anymore.

Sometimes when people become afraid
and start to lose their peace,
they remember a special person or persons
who practiced peace all the time

These special persons were nonviolent,
and they remembered to understand
and to forgive the people who hurt them.

Sometimes you can remember your peace
just by being able to understand and forgive.

Sometimes you can remember your peace
if you just stop and breathe quietly,
and listen very carefully to the peace
that is always inside of you.

There are many ways to remember your peace,
and maybe somebody you know and trust
can tell you more about the different ways
that they remember to keep their peace.

What is Peace?

Peace is a quiet thing
like watching clouds go by,
but it is not like being a quiet bug
that gets stepped on.

Peace is being really awake—
like listening real closely
in a deep green forest
and hearing the plants breathing
and the trees growing,
and the little animals moving their eyes around.

Peace is compromise and nonviolence.
Peace is not hurting anything or anybody—
not even the little animals in that beautiful forest,
or anything on our beautiful planet.
And not hurting others
is a way not to hurt ourselves.

And finally, peace is knowing
that we are all connected together—
through the sunlight and the starlight,
through the wind and the rain and the clouds—
to something much, much *bigger*
than we can ever even imagine.